This Book Belongs to:

Published in Nashville, Tennessee, by Tommy Nelson™, a division of Thomas Nelson, Inc.

Scripture quotations are from the *International Children's Bible, New Century Version*, copyright © 1986, 1988 by Word Publishing. Used by permission.

To contact the author, please write:

Liz Curtis Higgs
P.O. Box 43577
Louisville, KY 40253-0577

Library of Congress Cataloging-in-Publication Data

Higgs, Liz Curtis
The pine tree parable / by Liz Curtis Higgs; illustrated by Nancy Munger.
    p. cm.
Summary: A farmer and his wife, who grow trees to sell for Christmas, give their prized perfect tree to a poor family who cannot afford to pay for it.
  ISBN 0-8499-1480-9
  [1. Generosity–Fiction. 2. Trees–Fiction.]   I. Munger, Nancy, ill.
II. Title.
P27.H543955PAs   1997
[E]–dc21
                                                                            97-15570
                                                                              CIP
                                                                               AC

Printed in the United States of America

97 98 99 00 01 02 03 QPH 9 8 7 6 5 4 3 2 1

The Pine Tree Parable

by

Liz Curtis Higgs

Illustrated by Nancy Munger

Tommy
NELSON

Thomas Nelson, Inc.
Nashville

For Matthew and Lillian
—Liz Curtis Higgs

For Jessica and Joshua
—Nancy Munger Anderson

Every spring, the Farmer planted flowers.
Every summer, He grew fruits and vegetables.
Every fall, He harvested bright orange pumpkins.

Fresh Produce

As long as the earth continues, there will be planting and harvest.
Cold and hot, summer and winter." Genesis 8:22

And every day of every year, the Farmer grew the tallest, widest, biggest, greenest, loveliest crop of all . . .

. . .Christmas trees!

"He plants a pine tree, and the rain makes it grow."
Isaiah 44:14

The Farmer and His wife began planting seedlings when their children were small. Each year the family grew. So did the little pine trees.

The trees were quiet. The children were noisy. But the Farmer's wife loved everything that grew on the farm.

"Children are a gift from the Lord." Psalm 127:3

One chilly November day, the time finally came to sell the pine trees to the neighbors.

People bought the fine looking trees, which soon filled many homes with the fragrance of Christmas.

"Let each of us please his neighbor for his good, to help him be stronger in faith." Romans 15:2

But the Farmer's wife couldn't bear to part with one remarkable tree.

It stood very tall and perfectly straight. Its long branches danced on the wintry air.

The Farmer's wife hung a tag on the pine tree:
NOT FOR SALE. She added a shiny gold star on top.
Now the family could enjoy the tree day after
day, year after year, Christmas after Christmas.

*"So the tree was great and beautiful, with its long branches.
Its roots reached down to many waters." Ezekiel 31:7*

The next holiday season brought more neighbors to the farm. The perfect tree was taller than ever.

NOT FOR SALE

"So the tree was taller than all the other trees of the field." Ezekiel 31:5

Trees & Wreaths

When the neighbors asked, "Ooh, how much for this beautiful tree?" the Farmer's wife just smiled and shook her head. "Sorry. Not for sale."

"It cannot even be bought with the purest gold." Job 28:19

One Christmas Eve when the Farmer's children were children no longer, a family of three drove up in a rusty old truck.

Their clothes were patched, and their faces looked tired.

"You will always have the poor with you." Matthew 26:11

They trudged up and down a row of trees that no one else wanted. The trees had missing branches and crooked trunks.

Those trees were
free. They were the only kind of Christmas
tree the family could afford.

"The rich and the poor are alike in that the Lord made them all." Proverbs 22:2

The little child found her way to the tallest pine tree. She stood at the foot of it, looking up, up through the sweeping branches to the glistening star on top.

"Oh, my!" she sang out. "Can we buy this one?"

Her parents were embarrassed. They knew they could never afford it. The Farmer's family were also embarrassed. They knew, too.

But the little girl didn't know the cost. She only knew it was the most wonderful pine tree in the world. "Please?" was all she could say.

NOT FOR SALE

"It is sad when you don't get what you hoped for." Proverbs 13:12

The little girl was so poor yet so full of hope. What could the Farmer's wife say to her? What could she do?

"Whoever accepts a little child in my name accepts me." Matthew 18:5

The Farmer's wife took a deep breath. "I'm sorry," she said. "This tree is not for sale. But we'd like you to have it . . . as a gift."

Being kind to the poor is like lending to the Lord.
The Lord will reward you for what you have done. Proverbs 19:17

The little girl's parents could not speak a word. What a kind and generous gift! The Farmer's wife did not even know them. They were strangers.

The Farmer smiled at His wife. "Well done,
His smile seemed to say. "The gift is good."

Each one should give, then, what he has decided in his heart to give. . . .
God loves the person who gives happily." 2 Corinthians 9:7

As the Farmer took His saw to the bottom of the trunk, the child could not keep her joy inside. She leaped up and down. "Hooray! Hooray! The tree is ours!"

"When wishes come true, it's like eating fruit from the tree of life." Proverbs 13:12

The Farmer's wife watched her favorite pine tree as it fell to the snowy ground. Tears shone in her eyes. She brushed them away like snowflakes.

Yes, it was a great sacrifice. But it brought even greater joy.
Isn't that just like Christmas?

"You know that Christ was rich, but for you he became poor.
Christ did this so that by his being poor you might become rich." 2 Corinthians 8:9